Light-Hearted Verse by

JAMES MARSH

FROM *The* HEART

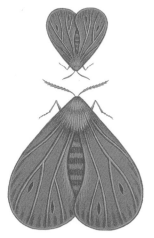

DIAL BOOKS · NEW YORK

SOFT-HEARTED

♥

I've found a perfect creature,
Instilled with feline grace;
Affection's fondly written
On her soft alluring face.

When we met I fell completely,
Hit upon by Cupid's dart,
I was bitten, I was smitten;
Then she made off with my heart.

LOVING HEART

♥

Whenever I see turtle doves
Intent to bill and coo,
I think of when we fell in love
And what we used to do.

Watching them becomes enthralling,
Perpetuating nature's calling.
You won't see them separated
Till loving hearts are consummated.

HEART'S DESIRE

♥

Here's a most romantic thing:
Dragonflies mate on the wing!
When secure in their embrace,
Procreation's taking place.

I'm captivated by this couple,
Slender-bodied, lithe, and supple.
(Although I try in my mind's eye,
My true love cannot make me fly!)

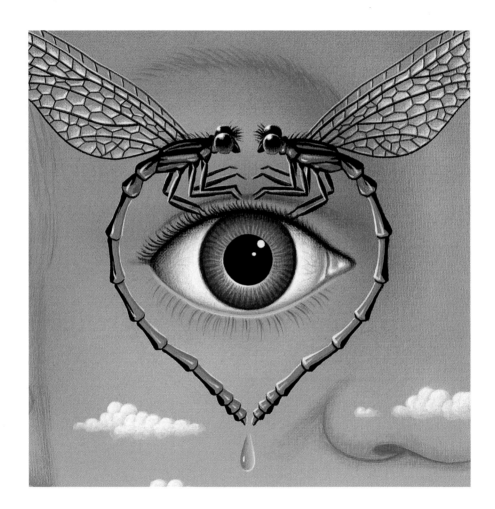

LIGHT-HEARTED

♥

Drawn to you like a moth to light,
Flickering and pining.
Through the gloom your love invites,
Toward you I'm inclining.

As a moth heads to the flame
Unaware of fire,
My heart's attracted just the same,
Guided by desire.

HEARTY BEAST

♥

Though I may look a little fat,
You love me still in spite of that.
I know that I can be a bore,
Yet you keep coming back for more.
Sometimes I can be a swine,
Even then you say you're mine.
It's obvious, to say the least,
That I have acted like a beast;
But you have turned my head around
And shown me where my heart is found.
That only leaves one thing to say…
I'm a hog for you in every way.

PRECIOUS HEART

Your heart is like a treasure,
A source of wealth to keep,
Impossible to measure…
Unfathomably deep.

Your love is like the ocean
That reaches deep inside,
My heart swells with emotion
And I can't stem the tide.

EMPTY-HEARTED

♥

Are you feeling empty-hearted,
On your own to sulk and mope?
Has your partner left you martyred,
Feeling there's no way to cope?

Keep your head and pillow parted,
Don't persist with sorrow's crown.
Resist dejection, get restarted,
Wear an optimistic frown.

WARM-HEARTED

Sheepishly I must reveal
Instinctively the way I feel.
This should come as no surprise,
I can't pull wool over your eyes.

Sheep can be romantic creatures
With all of their heart-warming features,
And so without much more ado
I must declare that I love ewe.

CHANGE OF HEART

♥

Whenever spring is close at hand,
The dark clouds roll away.
Bold blue skies awake the land
Where dormant flowers lay.

In summertime warm pleasant rays
Enrich the farmer's year,
And when it comes to autumn days,
Rich golden browns appear.

Whirling winter winds descend
To start the snowstorms blowing.
Heavy boughs begin to bend,
Their branches overflowing.

The charm of varied seasons
Enjoyed the whole year through
Cannot change my reasons
For pairing up with you.

WHOLE-HEARTED

♥

My mouth's agape, I'm going ape,
From your love there's no escape.
My heart's been in my mouth too long,
But now I simply can't go wrong.

Monkeylike, I jump with glee
And swing with joy from tree to tree.
I'm going nuts, I'm in a state
To learn that I am your prime-mate.

SWEETHEART

♥

Though rough on the eye,
The passionfruit
Is ever so sweet,
If not very cute.

It's a mistake
When choosing a lover
To judge any book
By what's on the cover.

Looks are deceptive.
It's no idle boast
That what's inside
Really matters the most.

HEART'S EASE

A self-indulgent, loving grin
Underlines my eyes.
I've got you underneath my skin,
Don't you realize?
I'm overjoyed, it's not a sin,
I won't apologize;
True happiness has fought to win
And brought me down to sighs....

HUNGRY HEART

♥

Your heart is like a lobster,
On the outside really tough,
But the inside's very tender
And I can't get enough.

Your heart is like a ripened fruit,
Refreshing, soft, and sweet,
When treated well, there's no dispute
It's good enough to eat.

Your heart is like a special dish,
A Cordon Bleu delight,
I can't resist, I only wish
To gorge my appetite!

LION HEART

Like the lion I have my pride,
But my main love I cannot hide.
I don't seek some tame mistress,
I'm looking for a lioness.
(Pause for thought, what's mine is yours,
This contract has no hidden clause.)
Act on instinct, choose your fate
And say that you will be my mate.

BIG-HEARTED

♥

At sunset on a balmy night,
When we are face to face,
My mouth drops open with delight
And love falls into place.

I'm bursting with desire for you,
With tons of love to share.
My heart beats fast enough for two
While passion fills the air.

FOR NATURE LOVERS EVERYWHERE

With special thanks to Nola for her inspiration

Published by Dial Books
A Division of Penguin Books USA Inc.
375 Hudson Street | New York, New York 10014

Printed in Hong Kong
by South China Printing Company (1988) Limited
First Edition
1 3 5 7 9 10 8 6 4 2
Library of Congress Catalog Card Number: 92-17912

The art was created with acrylic paints on canvas.
It was then color-separated and reproduced
as red, blue, yellow, and black halftones.